DISCARD

WOMEN
IN POLITICS

WOMEN IN THE WORLD™

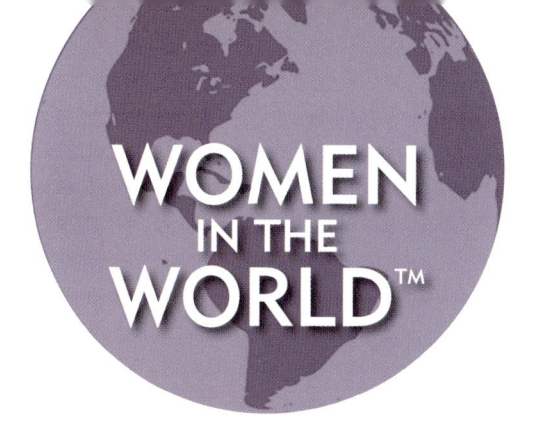

WOMEN IN POLITICS

AVERY ELIZABETH HURT

Rosen YA
New York

In memory of my dad and all those dinnertime political discussions

Published in 2018 by The Rosen Publishing Group, Inc.
29 East 21st Street, New York, NY 10010

Copyright © 2018 by The Rosen Publishing Group, Inc.

First Edition

All rights reserved. No part of this book may be reproduced in any form without permission in writing from the publisher, except by a reviewer.

Library of Congress Cataloging-in-Publication Data

Names: Hurt, Avery Elizabeth, author.
Title: Women in politics / Avery Elizabeth Hurt.
Description: New York : Rosen Publishing, [2018] | Series: Women in the world | Includes bibliographical references and index.
Identifiers: LCCN 2016056736 | ISBN 9781508174493 (library bound book)
Subjects: LCSH: Women—Political activity.
Classification: LCC HQ1236 .H885 2018 | DDC 324.082—dc23
LC record available at https://lccn.loc.gov/2016056736

Manufactured in China

CONTENTS

6 INTRODUCTION

10 CHAPTER 1
THE RADICAL NOTION

27 CHAPTER 2
WHY NOT RUN

45 CHAPTER 3
WHEN WOMEN RUN

62 CHAPTER 4
CRITICAL MASS

78 CHAPTER 5
WOMEN BELONG IN THE HOUSE . . . AND IN THE SENATE (BUT HOW DO WE GET THEM THERE?)

97 GLOSSARY

99 FOR MORE INFORMATION

103 FOR FURTHER READING

105 BIBLIOGRAPHY

109 INDEX

INTRODUCTION

When Hillary Clinton conceded her loss to Barack Obama in the 2008 Democratic primary election, she told her supporters, "Although we weren't able to shatter that highest, hardest glass ceiling this time, thanks to you, it's got about 18 million cracks in it. The path will be easier next time." The path wasn't easy; Clinton came heartbreakingly close in 2016 but was not quite able to win her bid for the nation's highest office. But by becoming the first woman presidential nominee of a major political party, she did put a lot more cracks in that ceiling.

A glass ceiling is a metaphor typically used to describe that level of achievement in business that women find it difficult, if not impossible, to get beyond. The metaphorical ceiling is glass because it is unacknowledged. People pretend that there is no barrier, that women can go just as high in their chosen professions as men do. But still, all too often,

INTRODUCTION

Luisa Dias Diogo became the first female prime minister of Mozambique in 2004. Under her leadership, the nation's economy and standard of living improved considerably.

women get to a certain level and can go no farther. Very few women head large corporations. But some do. In business that ceiling has been broken, at least occasionally. In the United States government, however, that ceiling is proving quite stubborn indeed. Almost one hundred years after women got the right to vote, still no woman has been elected president. The situation in the US Congress is not much better—21 percent of members of the Senate and 19.4 percent of members of the House of Representatives are female. In Canada (which briefly had a female prime minister in 1993) the percentage of female legislators is slightly higher at 26 percent.

Other countries have done better—but not that much better. Though women make up slightly more than half of the world population, they struggle to stay at 20 percent of the members of the world's legislative bodies. Worldwide there are fewer than twenty women heads of state. The reasons for this are not at all clear. Particularly in the West, there is no shortage of women who are more than qualified to run for and to serve in elected office. And when polled, voters say they are willing to elect women. Yet women are not even close to reflecting in government their numbers in the population. That 20 percent ceiling in legislatures is proving to be as stubborn as that highest glass ceiling.

INTRODUCTION

This text will take a look at many of the possible reasons women are less likely than men to run for office and the reasons it is still so difficult to persuade voters to support women when they do run for high office. We will see what happens when women do achieve power, in the United States as well as in other countries, and why electing more women may change the fate of the world—at the very least change the way the world is governed. We will close with a look at what it might take to finally break that highest glass ceiling and to get as many women as men in politics.

CHAPTER 1

THE RADICAL NOTION

"Feminism is the radical notion that women are people."
—Marie Shear

When John Adams was in Philadelphia in 1776 making plans for a new nation, he received a letter from his wife, Abigail. She wrote, "And by the way in the new Code of Laws which I suppose it will be necessary for you to make I desire you would remember the ladies, and be more generous and favourable to them than your ancestors." She continued to press her case on behalf of the women of the soon-to-be nation: "We are determined to foment

Unusual for her time, Abigail Adams believed that women should be educated and should help their husbands make decisions about family matters.

a rebellion, and will not hold ourselves bound by any laws in which we have no voice or representation."

John's reply to his beloved wife was an affectionate and amused comment about how "saucy" she was.

We can't be sure today whether Abigail was indeed just being saucy or if she was expressing a nascent feminism, truly calling for some kind of voice for women (if not true equality) to be spelled out in the constitution of the new nation. It is clear from her remarks, however, that she was using the very same argument that the colonists used against King George when they declared "no taxation without representation."

In any case, nothing in the constitution of the new country made mention of the rights of women; it did not give women the right to vote or to stand for elected office. That would be a long time coming.

FROM PHILADELPHIA TO SENECA FALLS

The "ladies" waited seventy-two years to foment their rebellion, but foment it they did. In 1848, abolitionists Elizabeth Cady Stanton and Lucretia Mott hastily organized the first women's rights convention in American history. The meeting was held in a small church in Seneca Falls, New York, and although only

One of the founding mothers of the women's rights movement, Elizabeth Cady Stanton began her life as an activist working for the abolition of slavery.

three hundred people attended (forty of them men, including freed slave and newspaper editor Frederick Douglass), the convention marked the beginning of a women's rights movement that is still ongoing today.

The official document stating the position and demands of the convention was called the Declaration of Sentiments. It was based on the US Declaration of Independence and demanded the recognition of women as equal members of society. The opening lines of the Declaration of Sentiments differed from that previous document by only two words—but crucial words they were: "We hold these truths to be self-evident: that all men **and women** are created equal; that they are endowed by their Creator with certain inalienable rights; that among these are life, liberty, and the pursuit of happiness." [Emphasis added.] But the truly radical notion in the Declaration of Sentiments came several paragraphs later in the document: "It is the duty of the women of this country to secure to themselves their sacred right to the elective franchise." Women were demanding the right to vote.

Though Seneca Falls kick-started the suffragist movement in the United States, it would be another seventy-two years before women made it into the voting booth. When the Nineteenth Amendment to the US Constitution was ratified in 1920, giving women the right to vote, only one of the women who signed the Declaration of Sentiments was still alive at that time.

THE RADICAL NOTION

MOTHER OF A MOVEMENT: SUSAN B. ANTHONY

Susan B. Anthony is often thought of as the mother of the women's rights movement in the United States. Like many suffragists, getting women the right to vote was not the only cause Anthony labored for, and she didn't wait until she could have her say in the voting booth before trying to make a difference in her society. As a teacher, Anthony worked to get equal pay for male and female teachers and a right to education for all children no matter what their gender or race. She was a staunch abolitionist and worked hard for African American rights. But she is best remembered as the mother of the women's right's movement, working to get women equal pay for equal work, the right of women to divorce men who were abusive, and of course, the right to vote.

In 1872, Anthony, along with fifteen other women, was arrested—for voting. Only Anthony was tried, and she hoped that her trial would be a test case. If her lawyers could prove her not guilty in a court of law, then women would have gained the right to vote in courts, without the necessity of a constitutional amendment. The judge, however, ordered the jury to find Anthony guilty of

(continued on the next page)

(continued from the previous page)

When Susan B. Anthony first became active in the temperance movement, she was not allowed to speak at rallies because she was a woman.

violating the law by voting when the constitution gave her no such right. Though she was found guilty, the trial was a turning point for the cause of women's suffrage. Anthony's legal and moral arguments and the courage she showed at her trial gave many people a new respect for the cause of women's suffrage.

Anthony died in 1906, fourteen years before the Nineteenth Amendment was ratified.

Charlotte Wood Pierce, who had been a young woman when she attended the Seneca Falls convention, was ninety-two years old in 1920 and, sadly, too ill to make it to the polls. But thanks to Pierce and her colleagues, women were at last able to have a voice and representation in the laws that they were bound to.

The movement for women's suffrage in Canada followed a similar pattern to that in the United States. The movement was driven in part by abolitionists and temperance leaders, and the campaign for the right to vote included demands for improvements in public health and equality in the areas of education and employment, as well as a movement to reduce violence against women. After a difficult struggle, Canadian women were granted the right to vote in federal elections in May of 1918, a little more than two years before US women achieved the same right.

Canada and the United States weren't alone in rethinking the role of women in political life—they weren't even the first. Most Western democracies had extended the right to vote to women by the early to mid-twentieth century. New Zealand was way ahead of the curve on women's suffrage, becoming, in 1893, the first country to allow women to vote. Australia followed suit in 1902. However, there were a few stragglers. Women in France did not get the vote until 1944, and in Italy not until 1945. Switzerland did not grant women the right to vote until 1971!

FROM THE VOTING BOOTH TO THE BALLOT

Though the right to vote and the right to run for office were understood to be a package deal, women had not been specifically prohibited from standing for office, and indeed women had run for national office in the United States well before they could vote. Elizabeth Cady Stanton ran for Congress in 1866, and in 1872, Victoria Woodhull ran for president

THE RADICAL NOTION

(though she was not yet thirty-five years old at the time and would have been ineligible to hold the office even if she had won the election—something she didn't come anywhere close to doing—because the US Constitution requires that presidents be thirty-five or older). But in any case, women seeking office, particularly national office, were rare and their candidacies were not taken

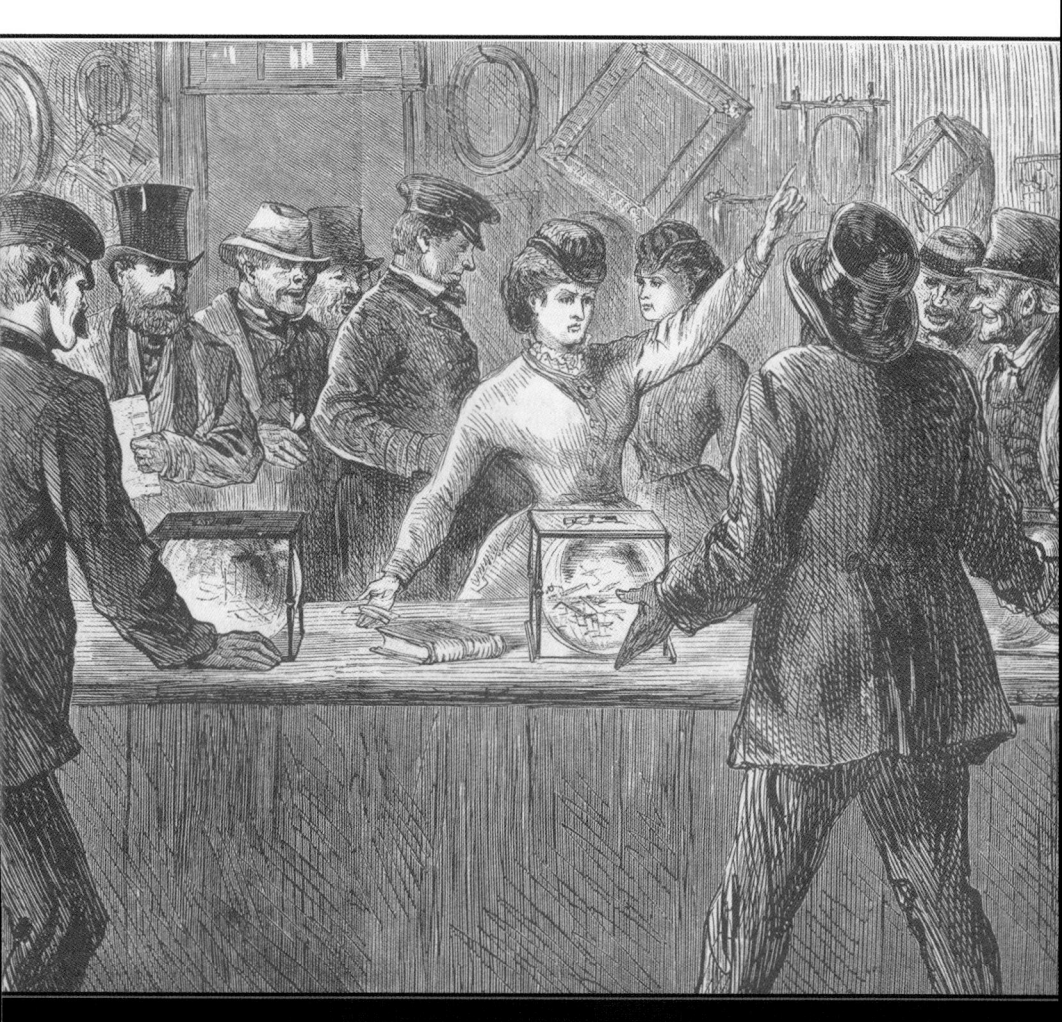

When Victoria Woodhull ran for president of the United States in 1872 she was not, because she was a woman, allowed to vote.

seriously by many voters. Perhaps most significantly, none of them were the candidate of a major political party, a fact that itself marginalized their candidacies. Without the support of a major party, women candidates were largely protest candidates and were often considered novelty candidates.

Once women got the right to vote in most nations, however, one might expect that women would have soon filled the halls of congresses and parliaments around the world. Unfortunately that has not been the case. Though women make up roughly 50 percent of the world's population, as of 2016 they accounted for just 22.8 percent of the members of legislative bodies worldwide, according to United Nations data. Again as of 2016, there were only ten women serving as heads of state worldwide, and as of 2015, only 17 percent of government ministers were women.

Canada is slightly ahead of the United States when it comes to women in high office. Twenty-six percent of its 2016 parliament was made up of women. Canada also elected its first female prime minister, Kim Campbell, in 1993, though she served only a few months. The United States, though coming close, has still not elected a woman to the executive office, and the number of women leaders in the United States is still discouraging. As of 2016, women accounted for seven cabinet-level positions, three of nine members of the Supreme Court, 19.4 percent of the members of the House of Representatives, and 20 percent of the Senate.

Kim Campbell, the first female prime minister of Canada, got her start in politics by serving on her local school board in Vancouver.

In the 2016 election, one more woman senator was added. The numbers are woeful in state governments as well. In the history of the United States, only thirty-seven women have ever served as governor of a state, and only twenty-five of those were elected in their own right (not replacing their husbands or coming to office by constitutional succession). In 2016, only six women were governors of US states and one was lost in the 2016 elections. Just how dismal are all these numbers? On a ranking of nations by the number of women in government, compiled by the Inter-Parliamentary Union, Canada ranks 64th, and the United States comes in at number 97 (on a list of 193 countries), twenty spots below the United Arab Emirates, which gave the vote to women only in 2006.

A LONG WAY, BABY

It is particularly odd that US women haven't seen the electoral success that women in many other nations have because now that American women can vote, they do. In the United States, women turn out to vote at rates 10 percent higher than men. But all those women at the polls aren't voting in a slew of women leaders. One obvious reason is that women run for office at much lower rates than men, but that simply raises the question of why women—who worked so hard and so long for the right to participate in government—are so reluctant to seek office. It has also taken US voters a

Hillary Clinton was the first female presidential candidate of a major party, but not the only recent woman nominee. Jill Stein was a Green Party candidate in 2012 and 2016.

surprisingly long time to warm to the idea of actually voting for women candidates, particularly for high office; the US presidency is proving to be a particularly tough goal. In 1937, 64 percent of people surveyed by research firm Gallup said that they would not vote for a woman president, even if she were "qualified in every other respect." By 1970, things hadn't changed much. Roughly two-thirds of Americans surveyed agreed that there wouldn't be a female president for "a long time," and, more significantly, that they were fine with that. However, by 2008, 95 percent of Americans were comfortable with the idea of a woman president in general, even if they weren't supportive of a particular female candidate. But as we saw in the most recent election, that highest of glass ceilings is proving a strong glass to break, and women aren't filling lower offices at anything like the rate you would expect in a world where virtually all voters say they are at least theoretically willing to have a woman in the highest office.

A 1970s-era advertising campaign aimed at women popularized the slogan, "You've come a long way, baby." But when it comes to being elected to political office, even four decades later, women still have a long way to go.

MYTHS AND FACTS

MYTH: Women tend to vote for women.

FACT: Women tend to vote for the party they prefer, rather than voting for women just because they are women. It has been argued that the reason Hillary Clinton lost the 2008 Democratic primary was a result of early losses in states such as Iowa and South Carolina, states where she lost the women's vote to Barack Obama by 5 percent and 24 percent, respectively.

MYTH: Outside of politics, gender equality has been mostly achieved in the United States.

FACT: Although women have made some impressive gains in recent years, they are still significantly underrepresented in management positions. According to a 2016 study by management consulting firm McKinsey & Company, in cooperation with LeanIn.org, a nonprofit organization designed to help women achieve their goals, only 19 percent of senior executive positions in US companies are held by women and women are in only 37 percent of lower-level managerial positions, despite being 47 percent of the workforce.

MYTH: Women voters are mostly interested in women's issues: paid family leave, subsidized child care, abortion rights, and equal pay.

(Myths and Facts continued on the next page)

WOMEN IN POLITICS

MYTHS AND FACTS

(Myths and Facts continued from the previous page)

FACT: In surveys asking about top priorities for the country, women typically list the same top priorities as men: the economy, health care, and terrorism.

MYTH: Women are less likely to run for political office because they are more focused on their families.

FACT: Women who are running for office are often asked far more questions about their family lives than their male counterparts—but that's more a perception of the voters (and perhaps the media) than the candidates. When news hit the stands that Hillary Clinton was going to become a grandmother, speculation and questions ran rampant. Would this affect her decision to run for president? But as far as we know, being a grandmother had no effect on Clinton's plans. Another potential candidate, Joe Biden, was not asked such questions, even though he had five grandchildren already! And in the end it was Biden who decided not to run because of family matters. The sad fact is that fewer women run for political office because they are simply not encouraged to do so. Nor are they among the first considered when a potential opening arises. Furthermore, studies show that even the most qualified women are under the impression that they are not, but the facts show that when they do run they do just as well at the polls as men and get about equal media coverage.

WHY NOT RUN?

CHAPTER 2

No matter how eager women are to vote for women candidates, they can't vote for women who aren't running. And women are far less politically ambitious than men. It is not entirely clear why women are hesitant to seek office, but there are a lot of theories and some data that might be able to help sort this out. A 2012 report by the Women & Politics Institute (WPI) identified several barriers to women seeking public office. Let's take a look at a few of them.

Women are more likely than men to think of the electoral environment as very competitive and biased against women, despite the fact that when women do run for office, they are as likely as men to win the offices they seek. In the WPI study, 62 percent of women said that in the area where they lived, congressional races were highly competitive, at least in lower offices. Only 50 percent of men surveyed viewed the electoral environment as competitive. The analysis of the study suggests that it is the perception of an uneven and highly competitive playing field that is distasteful to women, when according to the data that perception is not actually correct. Even if there is no bias against women in elections, a perceived bias can certainly discourage women from running. However, the notion that campaigns are more competitive for women is not necessarily a misperception. The fact that women win as often as men when they do run doesn't necessarily mean the process of winning isn't competitive. Women may be likely to win *even if the race is highly competitive*. A woman's disinclination to run could well be based on a distaste for competition, not a perceived inability to survive that competition.

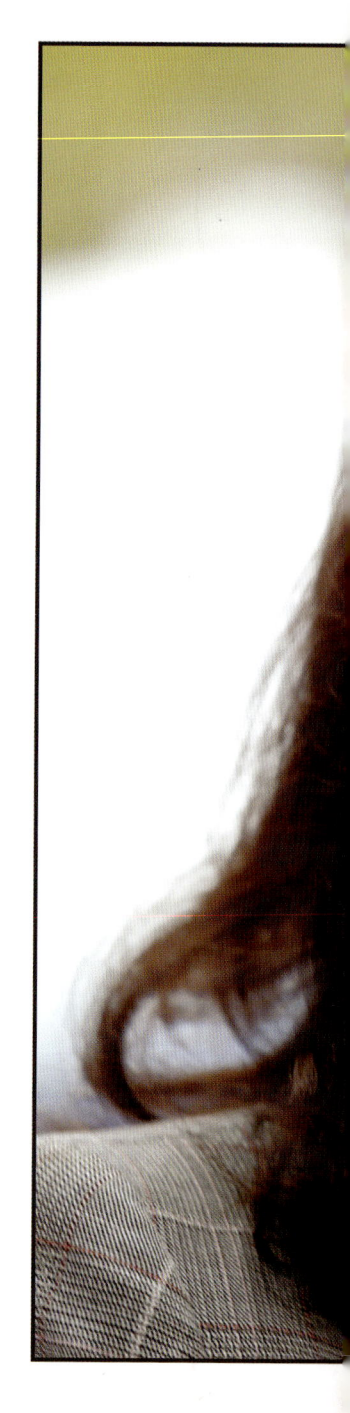

WHY NOT RUN?

Many think Senator Kamala Harris, the second black woman and first Indian American elected to the US Senate, has a chance of becoming the first female president of the United States.

Another factor that stops women from throwing their hats into elections, according to the WPI survey, is that women are less likely than men to consider themselves qualified to run. Even when women have roughly the same amount of experience conducting policy research, engaging in public speaking, and raising funds—all skills required for successful political campaigns—women rate themselves as less qualified than men rate themselves. Interestingly, even among men who do not consider themselves qualified for office, 55 percent of them have nonetheless considered a run. Among women who don't consider themselves qualified, only 39 percent have considered running. Men seem less likely to let a lack of qualifications keep them from jumping into the fray than women do. Women's lack of confidence and tendency to underestimate their own qualifications and undervalue their own experience keep the number of women seeking office low.

Some of the activities and experiences in a typical political campaign are also off-putting to many women. In her speech accepting the Democratic nomination for president, Hillary Clinton said, "Through all these years of public service, the 'service' part has come easier than

WHY NOT RUN?

Hillary Clinton proves that women can succeed in politics even if they are uncomfortable with the rough and tumble of public life.

the 'public' part." It seems that many women feel much the same way, being quite comfortable serving their communities, much less comfortable asking for the votes it takes to get them into positions where they can serve these communities. More than half of the women in the WPI survey said they were troubled by at least one of the activities involved in a political campaign. Campaign activities most likely to be unappealing to women were "soliciting campaign contributions," "potentially having to engage in a negative campaign," "loss of privacy," and "spending less time with family."

NOT THE FAMILY

The issue of time away from family is worth a closer look. The conflict between a woman's responsibilities to home and family and the demands of activities outside the home is one of the most discussed obstacles for women engaging in almost any kind of challenging and time-consuming endeavor because even today women are still responsible for the lion's share of child care and household tasks. According to a 2015 survey by the Pew Research Center, roughly six in ten respondents said that the mother takes a greater role in child care and managing kids' activities than the father does, while 41 percent said that the woman takes on a greater share of household responsibilities than her husband or male partner. But interestingly, this is not as great an obstacle as it is often thought to be. Despite time away from family being mentioned as one of the negative aspects of a political campaign, being responsible for the majority of child care and household chores does not seem to have a very significant effect on whether or not a woman considers running for office, according to the WPI survey. This probably shouldn't be very surprising. Women have been in the workplace for decades now, juggling families and jobs; the notion of balancing the demands of a family with the demands of public office is not that different from balancing the demands of a challenging job with the needs of a family.

And indeed, those women who already hold public office are demonstrating that even in the highest halls of power, working mothers are still mothers. In an article in *Pacific Standard* magazine, writer Nancy Cohen relates a story about US senator Kirsten Gillibrand, a mother of two from New York. Children are not allowed on the floor of the United States Senate, but according to the article, Gillibrand often casts votes from the door when her young boys are in the hallway during early evening votes. Women may not have made much progress when it comes to an equitable distribution of household chores, but they've

Kirsten Gillibrand holds her son Henry the day she is sworn into office as US Senator from New York.

definitely figured out how to balance work and family, even if it means doing the job from the doorway of the United States Senate.

THE STRUCTURE OF POLITICS

Although women certainly take into consideration all of the aforementioned factors when deciding whether or not to run for office, there are other, less personal factors that might limit women's involvement in politics. In many ways the structure of the political system has a lot to do with why—almost one hundred years after women got the right to vote—women's participation in politics in the United States lags so far behind women in other countries.

The United States' political system is, for the most part, a "winner take all" system. In most races, the field is narrowed down to two candidates, usually one from each major party, vying for only one available seat. The electoral systems of many other modern democracies have proportional representation. In these sorts of systems, districts are multi-seat, whereas in the United States congressional districts, for example, are mostly single-seat districts. In systems with proportional representation, the seats would be distributed proportionate to the votes each party received. If there were ten seats available and 40 percent of the voters cast ballots for the candidate running on Party A's ticket, then party A would get four seats, or 40 percent of the available seats. If Party B got 50 percent of the votes, then it would get 50 percent, or five seats. And Party C, which received a mere 10 percent of the vote, would still get one seat. There are several variations on the theme, and some systems can be quite complex, but this is the gist of it. Proportional representation has several advantages. It gives some say in governing to minority parties that are too small to ever prevail in a winner take all election, and it makes room for many voices in policy discussions.

MUTTI

Angela Merkel, the first woman chancellor of Germany, the most populous nation in the European Union (EU), confidently led the EU through one crisis after another as the "de facto" chancellor of Europe. The story of her rise to power is particularly satisfying because until she was thirty-five years old, she lived behind the iron curtain in East Germany, not allowed even to visit the West she would one day help guide through the tricky negotiations required to prevent another war like the one that led to the division of Germany into two countries, one free and one not.

In 2015, *Forbes* magazine named Merkel the second most powerful person in the world (second to then US president Barack Obama). Of course, she was clearly the most powerful *woman* in the world at the time.

Her popularity with the people of Germany waxed and waned over the years, but her steady hand, calm demeanor, and down-to-earth approach to governing has caused them to nickname her Mutti, the German word for "Mommy."

> Angela Merkel's experience growing up and living behind the Iron Curtain in East Germany no doubt influenced her commitment to freedom and opportunity for all people.

WHY NOT RUN?

37

Proportional representation is especially beneficial to women because in proportional representational systems, the majority parties are more eager to nominate candidates that have a broad appeal—and that means appealing to more women. And the more parties there are in the system, the more likely it is that some will put women up for office. Germany's political system has proportional representation. There, as of 2016, the Green Party has never won much more than 12 percent of the vote, but it has still had a voice in governing. In addition, Germany's Green Party has a rule that half the candidates that run as Green Party candidates must be men and half women, resulting in better representation of women in Germany's Bundestag (parliament).

Countries with parliamentarian systems are also likely to be friendlier to women candidates, for the same reasons. When no one party wins a straight majority in a parliamentarian system, coalition governments are often formed, making room for

WHY NOT RUN?

Muhterem Aras, a member of Germany's Green Party, is the first woman to be elected speaker of a state parliament in Germany.

representation from more less-powerful groups, such as women.

In the few cases where US states elect more than one representative per district, the pattern seems to hold as well. In these multi-member districts, consistently more women are elected than in states with single-member districts. The vast majority of US states have single-member districts. A move to more multi-seat districts might lead to more women in state and, eventually, national legislative bodies.

Another obstacle to women gaining equal representation is simply that men now dominate elected offices, and those who already have seats are more likely to retain them. There is a strong advantage to being incumbent. There is also the problem—often called a vicious cycle—that since there are few women in elected office, it seems that women can't be elected, so donors and political insiders are unwilling to support women candidates. Organizations such as Emily's List and the Women's Campaign Fund that support and raise money for women candidates are working to break this cycle, but it is taking some effort.

When it comes to the top job, other factors have contributed to the United States taking longer than some other modern democracies to elect a woman head of state. It is more difficult for a woman to become head of state in a presidential system, like the United States, than in a parliamentary system. In

EMILY's List

Former Speaker of the US House of Representatives Nancy Pelosi addresses the annual Emily's List Women in Power luncheon in March 2007.

parliamentary systems, voters elect a party rather than an individual. In order to become prime minister, a woman works with members of her party in a cooperative way to become the leader of the party, thus becoming the head of state if that party wins the national elections. In a presidential system, like in the United States, a woman has to win the votes of a majority of the voters. The fact that women are generally thought to be better at cooperation and consensus building makes it easier for them to get to the top in parliamentary systems.

YOU GO FIRST

As we have seen, organizations that work to recruit more women to run for public office often face an uphill battle; even convincing women that they are qualified to serve as elected officials takes some doing. However, once a few women are elected, more are likely to run for other offices. Amelia Showalter, director of digital

WHY NOT RUN?

Loretta Lynch, nominated by Barack Obama in 2014, was the first African American woman, the second woman, and the second African American to serve as US attorney general.

analytics for President Obama's 2012 campaign, analyzed thirty years of data for forty-nine states and found that when states elected women governors, they ended up with more women in their state legislatures in subsequent years. The same trend happens with other state offices as well; when women were elected to a high office, such as attorney general, more women ran for and were elected to lower offices. This may seem a little upside down at first glance. One might expect women to be elected to lower offices, that number to gradually increase, and then women would, after many years and much success in lower office, gradually climb the ladder to the top. After all, that's the way ladders are climbed: one rung at a time. But that's not how it works in politics. Women have to break a few glass ceilings first before other women are willing to follow. Showalter's research suggests that to get more women involved in all levels of government, we need to have a woman at the top. In the next chapter, we'll look at factors that keep voters from casting their ballots for a woman—and why they seem to be more reluctant to elect a woman the higher the office she is seeking.

WHEN WOMEN RUN

CHAPTER 3

The fact that women are hesitant to run for any political office until there are already women in higher office (governors, attorneys general, prime ministers, presidents) creates a bit of a catch-22 for women in politics. While American voters say that they are willing to elect women, the higher that office, the less willing they seem to be. Let's take a closer look at why it has been so difficult to get women in high office in the United States—and particularly why it is taking so long to elect a woman president of the United States.

A CRYING SCHOOLGIRL

Once in office, presidents are typically seen as solitary leaders, whereas heads of states in parliamentary governments are seen as more team leaders. Not only the process of gaining office, but the process of governing in a parliamentary system is seen as a matter of cooperation and consensus building—a job voters, and sociologists as well, seem to think is more suited to women than men.

In addition, the fact that in the United States the president is also commander in chief of the military may have something to do with voters' reluctance to elect a woman president. Even though the US military is open to women, it is still seen as a mostly masculine profession and there are few women in high command positions. In a paper called "A Woman in Charge of the Country? Women Prime

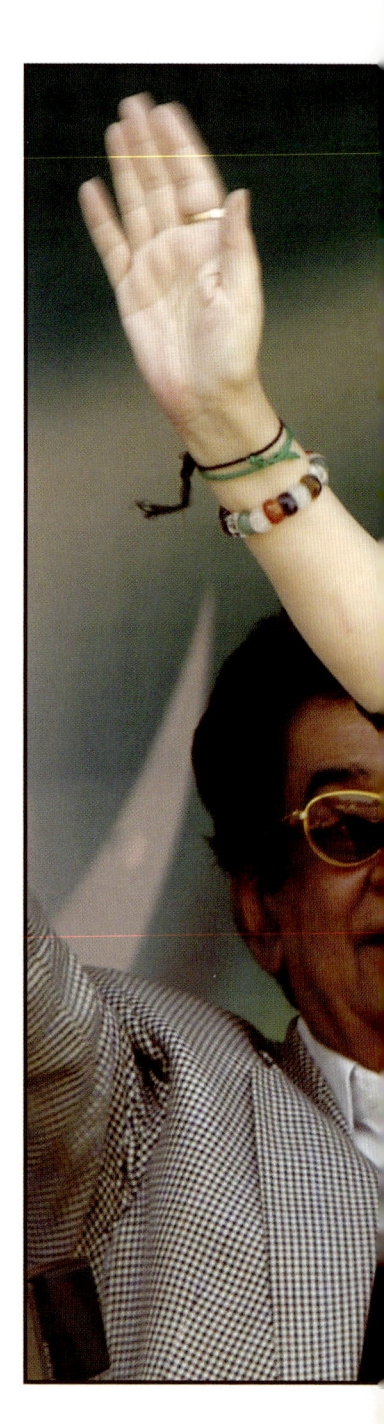

WHEN WOMEN RUN

Benazir Bhutto, twice elected prime minister of Pakistan, was the first woman to head a majority Muslim nation, and the only one to do so twice.

Ministers and Presidents—A (Not Quite) Global Phenomenon," political scientist Farida Jalalzai, points out that while there have been a scattering of women heads of state, few of them have led powerful countries. Canada, France, Germany, and the United Kingdom are the only G-8 nations (a group of eight industrialized nations that meet annually to confer about economic growth, global security, terrorism, and other matters) to have had women leaders, and the United Kingdom, France, India, Pakistan, and Israel are the only nuclear powers to have been lead by a woman. It's not clear why this might be the case, but the story of Jeannette Rankin might offer some insight to that question. Rankin was the first woman elected to the US Congress. She began serving in 1917, a little more than two years before ratification of the Nineteenth Amendment. (She was from Montana, one of only eleven states that had by that time given women the right to vote.) But the timing of her arrival on Capitol Hill is interesting in another way. She was a suffragist who ran on a platform that emphasized social issues. She was also a pacifist. On the very day she was sworn into office, President Woodrow Wilson asked Congress for a declaration of war against Germany. After much debate, Congress voted 373 to 50 to enter the First World War. Rankin was among those who voted no. "I want to stand by my country," she said as she cast her vote, "but I cannot vote for war." Even though forty-nine congressmen had voted against the war and one representative, Claude Kitchin of North Carolina, had wept as he argued against it during the debate, it was Rankin who was most severely criticized for her decision. A newspaper in her home state called her a "dagger in the hands of German propagandists" and a "dupe of the Kaiser." But perhaps more tellingly, the newspaper called her "a crying schoolgirl." It's possible that women have been seen as too weak or softhearted to take on a job that might require taking the nation to war. Almost exactly one hundred years after Rankin cast that vote, the first woman to come close to winning the presidency of the United States was often criticized for being too willing to pursue aggressive foreign policy. In any case, during her campaign for president, Hillary Rodham Clinton made much of the fact that she had been on the team that killed Osama Bin Laden, the terrorist leader behind the attacks on September 11, 2001. Women leaders have to disprove—perhaps even overcompensate for—the notion that women aren't tough enough to lead a powerful nation.

TWICE AS GOOD

Canadian feminist Charlotte Whitton is often quoted as saying, "Whatever women do, they must do twice as well as men to be thought half as good. Luckily, this is not difficult." This tongue-in-cheek formula

Charlotte Whitton was the first woman elected mayor of a major Canadian city. Though she was a powerful voice for women's equality, she was a social conservative.

has become an oft-repeated line in feminist circles. Of course, it's not clear if it is or ever was true, but there is a great deal of evidence that at least when it comes to politics, women have to work harder just to get the public's attention.

As in many other types of businesses, women are not equally represented in media jobs in the United States. Not even close. According to *The Status of Women in the US Media 2015*, a report by the Women's Media Center, a nonpartisan nonprofit dedicated to raising the visibility of women in media, men still dominate the press. Only 32.3 percent of bylines in the *New York Times* were women's, and other major newspapers had similar figures. Television anchors and on-air reporters were similarly likely to be men (with the notable exception of PBS, where both regular anchors, Judy Woodruff and the late Gwen Ifill, were women). When women do work on news stories, those stories are less likely (by roughly 35 to 65 percent) to be about politics. Women are far more likely to be assigned to cover education, lifestyle, and health. Does this have an effect on coverage of women candidates and women politicians? Maybe. In 2015, men accounted for roughly 74 percent of guests on major TV networks' Sunday morning news programs—the programs that offer regular in-depth coverage of politics and interview a wide variety of experts and pundits as well as politicians. In addition, according

WOMEN IN POLITICS

Prior to Ifill's 2016 death, Judy Woodruff (*left*) and Gwen Ifill (*right*) coanchored *PBS NewsHour*. They were the only all-female anchor team in broadcast journalism.

to the report, men still dominate news coverage, even when it is not about politics. This means that women, women's issues, and women candidates may not be as visible to voters as male candidates.

Not only do they have to work extra hard to turn the heads of the public, but women are faced with the frustration of struggling with their looks.

LOOK AT THAT FACE

Getting heard is not the only media challenge for women candidates. While both men and women candidates draw some attention for their looks (Donald Trump's hair and orangey tanned skin, for example, or Bernie Sanders's notoriously rumpled look), women endure far more scrutiny about their appearance than men do—and that scrutiny hurts them more.

WHAT COLOR IS YOUR PANTSUIT?

It may be hard to imagine now, but it was not until 1993 that women were allowed to wear pants on the floor of the United States Senate. These days, however, pants worn with a blazer and shell underneath is very common attire among women leaders. Angela Merkel wears that kind of outfit routinely, as does Theresa May, prime minister of the United Kingdom. Representative Nancy Pelosi and Senator Elizabeth Warren wear pantsuits often as well. But Hillary Clinton has really owned the style. Her Twitter bio reads in part, "pantsuit aficionado." At a fund-raising dinner she once joked that tuxedos are just formal pantsuits.

Like most clothes, pantsuits are powerful signifiers. Women began wearing pants in the early 1920s as a way of expressing their equality with men, though the practice did not become common until the 1970s. Jackets speak of something rather different: conformity. After all, pants and a jacket is utterly conventional business attire.

The pantsuit Clinton wore the night she accepted the Democratic nomination for president signified something else. White, purple, and gold were the

WHEN WOMEN RUN

British Prime Minister Theresa May arrives in India wearing a stylish pantsuit. Though May often wears pantsuits, she is also known for her stylish wardrobe.

official colors of the women's suffrage movement in the United States, and early fighters for the right to vote often wore white to marches and demonstrations to symbolize the purity of their goal. By wearing white on that historic night, and perhaps especially a white pantsuit, Clinton underscored the significance of her nomination and showed respect for the many women whose hard work made it possible for her to be there.

When Sarah Palin was running for vice president on the Republican ticket in 2008, her looks were frequently the subject of her coverage, generally in a positive way, but as we shall see, that's not much comfort to female candidates. The first female speaker of the US House of Representatives, Nancy Pelosi, got more media attention for her exceptionally stylish clothes than for many of her policy positions. And probably no candidate in the history of politics has been as scrutinized for her looks as Hillary Clinton. Comments on Clinton's looks have ranged from noting her "thick ankles" when she was First Lady and often wore dresses, to her habit, while secretary of state, of pulling her hair into a pony tail with a scrunchie and going without makeup. And of course, her penchant for pantsuits has been an ongoing source of fascination. It all seems rather silly and beside the point, but some research has shown that an emphasis on a candidate's appearance does have an effect on voters. A 2013 study funded by Name It Change It, a project working to end sexism in the media, found that descriptions of a female candidate's appearance whether negative, positive, or neutral, had a negative effect on voters' perception of her. In the study, male candidates did not suffer from coverage of their appearance, but any type of coverage of a female candidate's looks seemed to make voters see her as "less likable, less confident, less effective, and less qualified," the study found.

Sarah Palin, former governor of Alaska and 2008 vice presidential candidate, has not let being a mother—and now a grandmother—interfere with her political career.

57

It's not just in coverage of their appearance that women candidates have to overcome media hurdles that male candidate do not. When 2008 presidential candidate John McCain announced that Sarah Palin would be his running mate, some in the media questioned whether she could handle the job of vice president while being mother to five children. Palin was at that time, in addition to mother of five, governor of Alaska. When Clinton's daughter, Chelsea, became pregnant with her first child, some in the media speculated that being a grandmother might cause Clinton to drop her political ambitions. Women are also more likely than men to be deemed either physically or emotionally unfit for high office.

That attitudes like these are still prevalent may explain why despite the fact that voters say they are happy to elect a woman as president, they've never quite done so. In a forum on women in politics held at the Massachusetts Institute of Technology, writer Ellen Emerson White said, "I can't tell you how many times I've talked to someone … who says, 'I'd vote for a woman, just not that one.'"

IMPLICIT BIAS

It may simply be that the public has a hard time getting used to the idea of a woman in the role that has always been filled by a man. Yet the 2016 presidential campaign clearly demonstrated there is still a lot of misogyny in the electorate. In the first presidential debate of the 2016 campaign, Hillary Clinton said, "I think implicit bias is a problem for everyone." A batch of academic studies support this claim, finding that very nearly everyone has some degree of prejudice, whether they are aware of it or not. Clinton was talking about racial bias, but gender bias was certainly still evident in that election. Some of it was obvious—Trump supporters carrying signs saying "Trump that B****"—while some of it was much more subtle, such as repeated questions about whether or not Clinton had the stamina for the job. And of course, it wasn't just Clinton. Carly Fiorina, a candidate for the Republican nomination was the recipient of several vulgar sexist tweets, and Donald Trump made a not-so-veiled suggestion that debate moderator Megyn Kelly gave him tough questions in a debate because she was menstruating at the time. Of course, Trump is known for his lack of sensitivity to women. But other, less overt examples of sexist comments came from places where one would least expect it—supporting the argument for implicit gender bias. During a debate for the Democratic nomination, Clinton's opponent Bernie Sanders, a long-time progressive who has an excellent record on women's issues, said that Clinton would have to do more than "shout about" gun control, an almost certainly unintentional reference to the frequent criticism of

Before jumping into the 2016 presidential campaign, Carly Fiorina was CEO of Hewlett-Packard and the first woman to head a company listed on the Dow Jones Industrial Average.

Clinton's voice and the perception that she tends to shout a lot, but perhaps more seriously, a reminder that so often when women try to speak up (for themselves or others) they are perceived as shouting.

Women candidates face an interesting dilemma. While they are often ridiculed for being too soft or lacking the stamina for the job, they suffer equally when they appear to be ambitious or assertive, traits associated with men rather than women. "The more female politicians are seen as striving for power," psychologist Terri Vescio was quoted in an PBS article, "the less they're trusted and the more moral outrage is directed at them. If you're perceived as competent, you're not perceived as warm. But if you're liked and trusted, you're not seen as competent." Men do not seem to have this problem. And in the end, it is a problem for voters, who may have trouble hearing the message hidden beneath the sexist noise surrounding women candidates.

Despite all this, Hillary Rodham Clinton very nearly became the first woman president of the United States, so surely the day is not too far off when a woman will break that highest of glass ceilings in the United States. And when that does happen, a lot of things might change.

CHAPTER 4

CRITICAL MASS

Though it lags behind a lot of other countries when it comes to women in Congress, the United States is definitely making progress. In 2017, women made up 21 percent of Senate and 19 percent of the House of Representatives. Pretty dismal numbers, considering women are 51 percent of the population. But when you note that in 1950 there were only nine women in the House and only one in the Senate, and by 1990 that had gone up to twenty-nine women in the House and two in the Senate—twice as many!—it does look like progress, maybe even exponential progress. And it is. But it is still not enough. At this rate, it could take one hundred more years to reach gender parity (when the male/female ratio matches that of the population) in the United States Congress.

That may sound depressing, but there's some good news. Having women in power results in concrete change in government long before women achieve parity. "Critical mass" is a concept that was used initially in science as a way of describing the point at which a nuclear reaction can no longer be stopped, but the general idea is now used in other fields. In sociology, it refers to the point at which a minority begins to influence the policies and culture of a group that minority has gained access to. Critical mass in a group or organization is typically thought to be somewhere between 15 and 30 percent. Women have a way to go in the House, but at 20 percent of the Senate, they have reached a point where we ought to be seeing change. And we are.

PIZZA AND COMPROMISE

Each year the US Congress has to pass a set of bills to authorize funding for those government operations that are funded on a yearly basis. In 2013, right-wing factions of the Republican Party refused to pass the legislation necessary to keep key aspects of the government up and running unless that legislation included a provision that would eliminate funding for implementation of the Affordable Care Act (ACA), a health insurance program commonly known as

WOMEN IN POLITICS

US Senator Jeanne Shaheen holds a press conference during the 2013 government shutdown to discuss the effect of the shutdown on small businesses.

CRITICAL MASS

ObamaCare. Democrats refused to play ball; the popular health-care program wasn't on the table. Both sides drew lines in the sand and refused to even discuss any compromises that might avert a government shutdown. As a result hundreds of thousands of government employees were sent home from their jobs and more than a million others, including members of the military, continued working, knowing that their next paycheck would not arrive until the members of Congress managed to find a way out of the deadlock. Many government services and programs, like national parks, some federal food programs, NASA, and the national flu vaccine program, just to name a few, were affected.

About three weeks into the shutdown, most of the twenty women members of Senate met one evening in the offices of Jeanne Shaheen, a Democratic senator from New Hampshire. Over pizza, salad, and wine, they hammered out a deal that would get the government moving again. Each senator brought to the meeting ideas for compromise and a willingness to listen to the others' ideas. A Time magazine report of the meeting said that, "In policy terms, it was a potluck dinner." The next morning, the women presented the plan to the rest of the Senate, and the work to get the government back up and running was underway.

GETTING DOWN TO WORK

The 2013 government shutdown is just one example of what has come to be known as gridlock—the inability of government to get anything done because of an unwillingness of legislators to deviate from strict ideological positions. Women's style of governing—building consensus, making compromises, working with the opposing party, and yes, discussing it all over pizza and salad—has proven far more effective than filibusters and rule changes, power plays and grandstanding. When women get to Washington, they may not take the government by storm, but they do get things done.

Women don't just rise to the occasion to divert disaster. One key measure of the effectiveness of Congress is how much legislation gets introduced. By that measure, women are bringing their A game to Capitol Hill. In 2015, a group of Harvard researchers crunched the numbers and found that over the previous seven years in the US Senate, the average female senator had introduced 96.31 bills while the average male senator had introduced 70.72 bills. Perhaps more importantly, the women had far more cosponsors for their bills. The numbers were somewhat lower for the House of Representatives, but even in the lower chamber, women still did better, on average, than men in this benchmark of productivity. Women are also far more likely to introduce bipartisan legislation. In the years covered by the study, Susan Collins, Republican senator from Maine, sponsored 740 bills with sponsors from the opposite party. Many other female senators

Sen. Susan Collins, a Republican from Maine who was initially elected in 1997, often works with the opposition and votes across party lines to get legislation passed.

had hundreds of bipartisan bills to their credit as well.

When it comes to actually getting all that legislation passed into law, however, at least according to one study, it appears that women are more effective than men primarily when they are in the minority party—most likely because of the willingness to work with the opposition. Majority party women and majority party men see about the same amount of legislation enacted.

There is also a difference in the kinds of legislation women get behind. Women in power—both in the United States and in other countries—are far more likely than men to push progressive agendas. Women introduce more bills related to civil rights, the environment, education, health, and children's welfare than their male counterparts. In recent years women have shepherded through legislation that expanded funding of women's and children's health initiatives, provided maternity and family medical leave for federal workers, and strengthened equal pay laws.

That is not to say women legislators are focused entirely on women's issues. Women are also exceptionally good at managing very intricate legislation. The farm bill, for example, is a recurring piece of legislation that is known for its complexity—and sheer size. Senator Debbie Stabenow, a Democrat from Michigan and ranking member on the Senate Agriculture, Nutrition, and Forestry committee, gets the annual farm bill through the Senate by using something that has come to be known as the PTA method of legislating: break a big task into parts and delegate. This can't be done by grandstanding or overcontrolling but only by being able to work with others—a skill that the women in Senate cultivate, though it may come naturally to women. Vermont senator Patrick Leahy told Time magazine that Stabenow working on the farm bill was like "a big sister handing out chores."

Senator Lisa Murkowski in an interview on the Today show explained women's approach to solving the impasse over the debt (and no doubt it applies to their approach generally) by saying, "We tend to be pragmatic. This is not going to be a Republican Solution or a Democratic Solution. This is going to be a solution that is good for the country."

And food helps, too. Seriously. That late-night pizza and wine meeting about how to get the government up and running wasn't an anomaly. The women in Congress have mentor lunches and regular dinners together, often at one of their homes. While many of the lunches are working meetings, the ground rules during their regularly scheduled dinners are no talking about politics. Food may seem as extraneous to the process of governing as clothes are, but maybe it's not. Getting to know one another and forming bonds of respect and friendship over meals provides a firm ground for working together at times when the environment is not so amiable and the stakes are much higher.

WHAT'S WITH RWANDA?

When you take a look at nations in order of the percentage of women in parliaments, it sort of jumps out at you that perched at the top of the list is Rwanda, a country that only slightly more than twenty years ago saw the end of a genocide in which an estimated one million people were killed. Yet today, Rwanda has a stable government and a growing economy and is the only country in the world with more female politicians than male ones. So how did they do it? And how's that working for them?

Part of the reason is that after the genocide, more than 70 percent of the surviving population was female. And those women took

CRITICAL MASS

After the civil war in Rwanda, women like MP Faith Mukakalisa stepped up to help rebuild the nation. Women are still in the majority in the government there.

on the responsibility of rebuilding their nation. Because the civil war was a consequence of a what Juliana Kantengwa, a member of the Rwandan parliament, described as a "divisive and destructive culture," the women leaders worked especially hard to put, in Kantengwa's words, "inclusiveness and equality" at the heart of the rebuilt nation.

In the twenty-odd years since the end of the war, women who came to power in the post-genocide era were determined not to let gradual gender rebalancing of the population cost them the power they'd gained. They appointed or helped elect women to other senior government positions and many lower ones. Half of the country's Supreme Court justices are women.

Rwanda's women have implemented a great deal of social change as well. For the first time, boys and girls attend primary and secondary schools in equal numbers, and women are allowed to own and inherit property. And perhaps most important of all, the streets that once ran with blood are safe.

BANKING ON A WOMAN LEADER

While women in the US Congress are battling gridlock and pushing through progressive agendas and complicated farm bills, women heads of state around the world are having an interesting effect on the economies of the countries they lead. Professor Katherine Phillips

The sixty-five woman Democrats elected to the 114th Congress's House of Representatives represent the largest number of women in a party caucus in the history of the US Congress.

of Columbia University led a team of researchers who found that for countries with ethnically diverse populations, electing a female leader correlated with a significant increase in growth of GDP (gross domestic product, a measure of the economic health of a nation) compared with countries with male leaders. It's difficult to say why this is the case, but the authors of the study suggested that it was because women's more inclusive leadership styles bring more people into the economy.

WOMEN IN POLITICS

Angela Merkel has a degree in physics and a doctorate in quantum chemistry. Some suggest that her scientific training explains her systematic approach to governing.

The researchers suggest another fascinating possibility as well: perhaps because the very fact of electing a woman is a sign of change, the mere presence of a woman in a high leadership position motivates other marginalized groups to more fully participate in the economy, thus leading to economic growth. That's not unlike the effect, noted in chapter three, that more women will run for lower offices once a few women have been elected to high office. (Interestingly, Phillips also noted that companies with women at the top tend to be more innovative and profitable as well.)

Germany under the leadership of Angela Merkel, its first female head of state, has been described as being in something of a golden age. Germany's economy has improved dramatically under Merkel's leadership, and Merkel has guided the European Union through a series of financial crises. Germany has changed in other ways under Merkel's leadership as well. Of course, there are many factors that affect the economic conditions of a nation, and the happiness and well-being of its citizens are dependent in no small part on those economic conditions. Though it can be hard to determine the causes of a change in the mood of a nation, and even harder to evaluate the happiness of a group of people, it is certainly no stretch to say that a country with more equality and more opportunity for everyone is a better place to live. When women get power, things do change, and mostly, it seems, for the better.

10 GREAT QUESTIONS TO ASK AN ACTIVIST FOR WOMEN IN POLITICS

1. I think I might be interested in running for office one day. Will it help me to get involved in student government now?

2. I could never run for office, but I would like to be involved in the political system in other ways. What are my options?

3. Can I start now to help get more women elected, even though I'm not yet old enough to vote?

4. If there are so few women in politics, how can we ever hope to make a difference?

5. Do we really need more women in politics? It seems like things are getting better for women anyway.

6. When women have important jobs in government, how can they find enough time to spend with their children?

7. I'm a guy, but I definitely see the importance or gender equality and balanced representation. Can I get involved with this issue even though I'm not female?

8. I want it all. I want to help run the world and also have a family. Is that even possible?

9. If other countries are so far ahead of the United States and Canada when it comes to women in government, does that mean that we need to change our forms of government to systems that are friendlier to women?

10. If I think I might one day want to work in government, either as an elected official or in some other capacity, what subjects should I concentrate on in school?

CHAPTER 5

WOMEN BELONG IN THE HOUSE...AND IN THE SENATE (BUT HOW DO WE GET THEM THERE?)

In the early days of the modern feminist movement, a popular T-shirt slogan played on the then widely accepted notion that women are more suited for raising families than taking part in politics. The slogan read, "Women belong in the house—and in the Senate." These days most people seem to agree. But how do we get them there? As we saw in chapter two, women have an easier time coming to power in countries with parliamentary systems and of being elected in countries and districts with proportional representation. But this does not address the problem of persuading women to run in the

WOMEN BELONG IN THE HOUSE...AND IN THE SENATE (BUT HOW DO WE GET THEM THERE?)

first place. Many organizations exist solely to recruit women candidates and train them in the art and science of campaigning, but they face difficulties just getting women in the pipeline. What can they learn from countries with better track records?

QUOTAS

When Justin Trudeau became prime minister of Canada in 2015, he announced that 50 percent of his cabinet would be women. At that time in the United States, only seven of twenty-two cabinet positions, just under a third, were filled by women. (Though to be fair, President Bill Clinton's cabinet was 40 percent women—the closet we've been so far to parity in the cabinet. Choosing a half-female cabinet is more than a gesture toward gender equality (though it is certainly a savvy political move). Having more women cabinet members (and more people of color as well—in short a cabinet that more nearly reflects the population) allows a president or prime minister to hear the voices and points of view of the entire spectrum of the nation that president serves. It can also help recruit women to politics. Women cabinet members get high-level government experience and contacts, and the voters get used to seeing women in these powerful jobs, making the idea of a woman in office seem less unusual. Hillary Clinton's tenure as secretary of state

WOMEN IN POLITICS

When Canadian Prime Minister Justin Trudeau (*pictured*) was asked why he appointed a gender-balanced cabinet, his answer was, "Because it's 2015."

WOMEN BELONG IN THE HOUSE...AND IN THE SENATE (BUT HOW DO WE GET THEM THERE?)

was one of the primary arguments in establishing her qualifications for the presidency.

The idea of forced parity—women are roughly half the population, so we should make sure they make up half the leadership—does not fit well with the United States' more laissez-faire attitude. But other countries have embraced the idea—not just with cabinet posts, but with candidates. According to a 2015 study in the journal *Legislative Studies Quarterly*, as of 2010 more than sixty nations had included gender quotas in their electoral laws or constitutions and several others were considering it. Critics of gender quotas point out that simply having more women on ballots is not enough to ensure parity in office. In Brazil, for example, 30 percent of candidates must be women, but female candidates there are not as likely to win office as their male counterparts. Even if the United

FEMALE FIRSTS

Glass ceilings aren't broken overnight. There were many firsts in the United States leading up to Hillary Clinton's nomination.

Here are a few:
- *First woman to run for Congress*: Elizabeth Cady Stanton ran as an independent in New York in 1866. She won 24 of 12,000 votes cast.

- *First woman elected to Congress*: Jeannette Rankin of Montana in 1916.

- *First woman to serve in the Senate*: Rebecca Felton of Georgia. She was appointed in 1922 to fill a vacancy but served just twenty-four hours.

- *First African American woman elected to Congress*: Shirley Chisholm of New York in 1968. In 1972, she ran for the Democratic nomination for president. She served seven terms in the House of Representatives.

(continued on the next page)

WOMEN BELONG IN THE HOUSE...AND IN THE SENATE (BUT HOW DO WE GET THEM THERE?)

Shirley Chisholm said that she ran for president in 1972, even against such long odds, so that other women and minorities would be inspired to run for high office.

(continued from the previous page)

- *First woman elected to the Senate*: Hattie Wyatt Caraway of Arkansas. She was elected in 1932 after stepping in to fill her husband's seat after he died. She was re-elected in 1938.

- *First African American woman elected to the Senate*: Carol Moseley Braun of Illinois in 1992. She ran for the Democratic nomination for president in 2004.

- *First openly gay woman elected to the Senate*: Tammy Baldwin of Wisconsin in 2012. Baldwin had previously served seven terms in the House of Representatives.

States, where women candidates tend to do roughly as well as men (at least when running for lower offices), many people think that having quotas could result in less qualified candidates, though the data in the above study does not support this. However, even if women candidates are equally qualified, quota systems may give the impression that they are not, but have achieved their success because of quota requirements. When it comes to getting more women

WOMEN BELONG IN THE HOUSE...AND IN THE SENATE (BUT HOW DO WE GET THEM THERE?)

in office, however, quotas are simply not the only game in town.

TRAIN 'EM UP

As part of its commitment to ending all forms of discrimination and supporting women's rights to participation in all areas of public life, the United Nations (UN) has developed several programs for training women political candidates and encouraging advocacy for gender equality. The results of these training programs have been positive. After the UN provided training to nine hundred female candidates in Kenya, the number of women legislators in that country more than doubled in the 2013 elections. Similar programs in Timor-Leste have resulted in 38 percent women representation—more than the 30 percent quota required there. In Zimbabwe, a UN-supported gender-equality lobbying group known as the Group of 20 was instrumental in passing a constitution that is strong on women's rights, leading to a jump from 17 percent to 35 percent female representation.

Organizations in the United States also see the need to train women candidates. Better training of women candidates could potentially erase the reluctance of US women to run for office because they do not feel qualified (even when they are) or because they perceive the competition to be stiffer than it is.

WOMEN IN POLITICS

Indian-born Kalpana Rawal retired in 2016 as deputy chief justice of the Supreme Court of Kenya. She was the first woman to set up a private law practice in Kenya.

WOMEN BELONG IN THE HOUSE...AND IN THE SENATE (BUT HOW DO WE GET THEM THERE?)

Emily's List, one of the first and most well-known organizations that supports women candidates, is a US organization dedicated specifically to electing more pro-choice Democratic women, and it's been quite successful at recruiting and training, as well as raising money and attention for its candidates. Other groups have a wider brief—to get more women of any party or policy into office. The nonpartisan Center for American Women in Politics (CAWP), at Rutgers University, is a research organization dedicated to education about women in politics and to enhancing women's leadership. It sponsors Ready to Run, a national network of nonpartisan training programs for women candidates. Vote Run Lead (VRL), an organization started in 2014, works specifically to get more women candidates on the ballots at the local level. After actively recruiting women candidates, VRL provides them with both online and in-person training sessions about how to launch, fund, and run a campaign for office. A similar organization, She Should Run, has a variety of initiatives (some of them with a clear sense of humor), including an online incubator that helps to recruit and prepare women for the campaign trail. NOBEL women, National Organization of Black Elected Legislative Women, works especially to recruit and train black women for elected office. With so many groups working to help women overcome the difficulties they have in running for office, the momentum is gradually shifting. And now after Hillary Clinton's oh-so-very-close bid for president, that momentum should build even more.

However, if the country is going to achieve gender parity in politics—particularly at the national level—these organizations can't limit their training to older women who are already well positioned for a run. They'll have to train young women and girls. Many if not most of these organizations are doing that, at least a little bit. Of course with younger women, the focus is not on how to structure a campaign organization, solicit donations, or work with party leaders. The emphasis is instead on building leadership skills and starting to see themselves as one day becoming society's leaders. CAWP's Teach a Girl to Lead (TAG) initiative provides schools and community organizations with lesson plans and other materials they can use in developing leadership program for girls. But perhaps more importantly, on the theory that you have to see one to be one, TAG works to expose young people to women in leadership positions, both past and present, in order to expand their ideas about who can lead.

WHAT DOES IT TAKE?

Plenty of studies have been done on how many women are in power and what they do when they get there, but there is far less research on the paths women take to the top of their governments. Susan Madsen, a researcher at Utah Valley University, wanted to know what female heads of state had in common. After interviewing several women leaders in China and the United Arab Emirates, she found some interesting similarities, despite the fact that these women grew up and governed in different—even vastly different—cultures. The one thing said by every woman Madsen spoke with was that she developed her ability to form and share opinions during dinner time conversations with her family. The women's fathers valued education and in some cases went to a great deal of trouble to make sure their daughters as well as their sons were educated. Their fathers brought home books for their daughters to read and encouraged political conversations and debate. Even when their daughters disagreed with them, they were allowed to express their views. It wasn't just fathers, though. The mothers of these future leaders were strong leaders in the family, setting an example for their daughters in

(continued on the next page)

WOMEN IN POLITICS

(continued from the previous page)

The first female president of Chile, Michelle Bachelet was the first popularly elected South American president whose political career was established independently of her husband.

the home, even if there weren't many such examples in their society.

Madsen also discovered that women tend to take different routes to power than men do. Rather than aiming directly for the top from the beginning, women are more likely to begin by working on local, grassroots issues, often coming to politics via a benevolent cause or career—much the way Hillary Clinton began her career working for children's rights advocate Marian Wright Edelman, or Michelle Bachelet, president of Chile, who studied medicine so that she could help people deal with pain.

BUT I MEAN, LIKE YUCK

The current generation of women politicians who are breaking glass ceilings grew up in a much different political world than today's young people live in. Though women were even more vastly underrepresented in elected office, and women faced worse discrimination and more severe pay inequity, previous generations saw politics as a viable route to creating a better world—and many of them were engaged, even excited by politics.

In the 1960s and 1970s, working for political causes—and aspiring to political office—was commonplace. Hillary Clinton has been accused (and the fact that the word here is "accused" is itself telling) of running for the presidency all her life. She did, after all, give an address at her own graduation from Wellesley College (the first student to speak at a Wellesley commencement ceremony). Her address was not only a first, she used her time at the podium to challenge the comments of the previous speaker, United States senator Edward Brooke, who had just claimed that social protest was both wrong and unnecessary. Clinton (then Hillary Rodham) countered with the now-famous statement (speaking on behalf of her entire graduating class), "We feel that for too long our leaders have viewed politics as the art of the possible. And the challenge now is to practice politics as the art of making what appears to be impossible possible." At that time, 1969, a woman as presidential candidate of a major political party appeared quite impossible.

There was no doubt that social change was already on Hillary Rodham's agenda, whether she did it from the Oval Office or somewhere else. However, today's young women (and young men, too, for that matter) are not nearly so politically energized. In fact many of them seem totally turned off by politics. In the 2015 book *Running from Office,* political science professors Jennifer Lawless and Richard Fox describe their survey of more than four thousand high school and college students. When asked if they might be

Hillary Rodham in May 1969, when she was a senior at Wellesley College. Clinton began preparing for her political career when she was still a young woman.

interested in running for political office one day, 89 percent of them said "no." Lawless and Fox followed up with more than one hundred in-depth interviews and discovered that today's polarized, dysfunctional, and mean-spirited political climate is responsible for turning off young people at a historic rate. There was a time, not that long ago, when young people truly believed that they could make a difference by getting into politics, that if you wanted to make the world a better place—however you conceived that better place to be—politics was the way to do it. Now they see a political system so dysfunctional that they are beyond "why bother," and already onto "not in a million years."

But as the women in the US Senate and women leaders around the world have shown, getting involved in politics really can change things—if the people who get involved are the ones who care about making that change. But that will almost certainly take more women.

WOMEN BELONG IN THE HOUSE...AND IN THE SENATE (BUT HOW DO WE GET THEM THERE?)

Fu Ying, the vice minister of the Foreign Ministry of the People's Republic of China, is only the second woman ever to serve in that position.

Although Hillary Clinton didn't quite break that highest of glass ceilings, by coming so heartbreakingly close, she has surely shown other women and girls what a female president can—and will one day—look like. For that to happen, though, women and especially young women and girls must not give up, must not begin to believe that it can never happen. They need to continue the work begun by Clinton and so many other women like her, from the halls of the US Senate to local school boards, and start preparing for the journey to leadership. In some ways, the fate of the world may depend on it.

GLOSSARY

ABOLITIONIST Someone who supports the ending of a practice or institution, especially slavery.

CABINET A group of high-level government officials who run departments and advise heads of state.

CHANCELLOR The head of government in some countries, for example Germany and Austria.

COSPONSOR In Congress, a person who adds his or her name to another person's bill to show support for that bill.

EXPONENTIAL Characterized by a rapid increase—an increase that becomes more rapid over time.

FILIBUSTER An attempt to delay or prevent action on legislation by taking up time on the floor with long speeches.

FOMENT To agitate or incite an action or attitude, often civic unrest.

FRANCHISE The right to vote.

GENOCIDE The mass slaughter of people belonging to a given racial, political, or cultural group.

IMPLICIT BIAS Unconscious or unacknowledged prejudices, judgments, or beliefs.

INCUMBENT A person currently holding office.

LAISSEZ-FAIRE A policy or practice that involves letting things take their natural course without unnecessary interference from government or other authority.

MINISTER A government official who heads a department of that government.

MISOGYNY A dislike or prejudice against women.

NONPARTISAN Not belonging to or supportive of the policies of a particular political party.

PARITY Being equal, especially in terms of status or pay.

PARLIAMENT A body of lawmakers.

SIGNIFIER Something that represents, symbolizes, or stands for something else.

SUFFRAGE The right to vote.

SUFFRAGIST Someone who works to get the right to vote for a group that does not have it (historically women).

TEMPERANCE The practice of refraining from drinking alcoholic beverages.

Center for American Women in Politics
191 Ryders Lane
New Brunswick, NJ 08901
(848) 932-9384
Email: cawp.info@eagleton.rutgers.edu
Website: http://www.cawp.rutgers.edu
A part of the Eagleton Institute of Politics, CAWP is dedicated to promoting greater knowledge and understanding about women's participation in politics and government and to enhancing women's influence and leadership in public life.

Equal Voice
116 Albert, Suite 810
Ottawa, ON K1P 5G3
Canada
(613) 236-0302
Email: nfo@equalvoice.ca
Website: https://www.equalvoice.ca/index.cfm
A national, bilingual multipartisan organization dedicated to electing women to all levels of political office in Canada.

Girls Incorporated
120 Wall Street, 3rd Floor
New York, NY 10005
(212) 509-2000
E-mail: communications@girlsinc.org

Website: http://www.girlsinc.org
Girls Incorporated is a national nonprofit youth organization dedicated to inspiring all girls to be strong, smart, and bold.

Girls in Politics
1200 G Street NW
Washington, DC 20005
(202) 660-1457 ext. 2
Email: info@girlsinpolitics.org
Website: http://www.girlsinpolitics.org
An initiative of the Political Institute for Women, GIP introduces girls ages eight to seventeen to politics, policy, the work of the US Congress, parliamentary governments, and the United Nations.

National Council of Women of Canada
Le Conseil National des Femmes du Canada
PO Box 67099
Ottawa, ON K2A 4E4
Canada
(902) 422-8485
Email: pres@ncwcanda.com
Website: www.ncwcanada.com
This is an organization of women working to bring to the attention of government issues that affect families and communities.

FOR MORE INFORMATION

National Organization for Women (NOW)
1100 H Street NW, Suite 300
Washington, DC 20005
(202) 628-8669
Website: http://www.now.org
The largest organization of feminist activists in the United States, NOW works to eliminate discrimination and harassment; secure abortion, birth control and reproductive rights for all women; end all forms of violence against women; eradicate racism, sexism, and homophobia; and promote equality and justice in our society.

Running Start
1310 L Street NW
Washington, DC 20005
(202) 223-3895
Email: info@runningstartonline.org
Website: http://runningstartonline.org
Running Start is an organization that educates young women about politics and gives them the skills they need to be leaders.

Teach a Girl to Lead (TAG)
191 Ryders Lane
New Brunswick, NJ 08901
(732) 932-6778

Email: tag@eagleton.rutgers.edu
Website: tag.rutgers.edu
A project of the Center for American Women in Politics, TAG helps young people rethink leadership so that they can imagine women in leadership roles.

Younger Women's Task Force
American Association of University Women (AAUW)
1310 L St. NW, Suite 1000
Washington, DC 20005
(202) 785-7700
Website: http://www.aauw.org/membership/ywtf/
The Younger Women's Task Force is a nationwide diverse and inclusive grassroots movement dedicated to organizing younger women and their allies to take action on issues that matter most to them.

WEBSITES

Because of the changing nature of internet links, Rosen Publishing has developed an online list of websites related to the subject of this book. This site is updated regularly. Please use this link to access this list:
http://www.rosenlinks.com/WITW/politics

FOR FURTHER READING

Alexander, Heather. *Who Is Hillary Clinton?* New York, NY: Grosset & Dunlap, 2016.

Bausum, Ann. *With Courage and Cloth: Winning the Fight for a Woman's Right to Vote.* Washington, DC: National Geographic Children's Books, 2004.

Blumenthal, Karen. *Hillary Rodham Clinton: A Woman Living History.* New York, NY: Feiwel & Friends, 2016.

Bolden, Tonya. *33 Things Every Girl Should Know About Women's History: From Suffragettes to Skirt Lengths to the E.R.A.* New York, NY: Crown, 2002.

Cooper, Ilene. *A Woman in the House (and Senate): How Women Came to the United States Congress, Broke Down Barriers, and Changed the Country.* New York, NY: Abrams, 2014.

Goodman, Susan E. *See How They Run: Campaign Dreams, Election Schemes, and the Race to the White House.* New York, NY: Bloomsbury, 2012

Hollihan, Kerrie Logan. *Rightfully Ours: How Women Won the Vote.* Chicago, IL: Chicago Review Press, 2012.

Jacobs, Tom, and Natalie Jacobs. *Every Vote Matters: The Power of Your Voice, from Student Elections to the Supreme Court.* Golden Valley, MN: Free Spirit Publishing, 2016.

Justice Learning. *The United States Constitution: What It Says, What It Means.* New York, NY: Oxford University Press, 2005.

Lowery, Zoe. *Democracy.* New York, NY: Rosen Education Service, 2014.

Thimmesh, Catherine. *Madame President: The Extraordinary, True (and Evolving) Story of Women in Politics.* Boston, MA: Houghton Mifflin, 2004.

Columbia Business School. "When Women Rule, Nations Prosper." February 21, 2014. https://www8.gsb.columbia.edu/articles/ideas-work/when-women-rule-nations-prosper.

The Elizabeth Cady Stanton & Susan B. Anthony Papers Project. "Declaration of Sentiments and Resolutions." Retrieved September 2016. http://ecssba.rutgers.edu/docs/seneca.html.

Fitzpatrick, Ellen. *The Highest Glass Ceiling: Women's Quest for the American Presidency.* Cambridge, MA: Harvard University Press, 2016.

Lawless, Jennifer L. "It's the Family Stupid? Not Quite... How Traditional Gender Roles Do Not Affect Women's Political Ambition." Brookings, July 17, 2104. https://www.brookings.edu/research/its-the-family-stupid-not-quite-how-traditional-gender-roles-do-not-affect-womens-political-ambition.

Lawless, Jennifer L., and Richard Fox. *Running From Office: Why Young Americans Are Turned Off to Politics.* New York, NY: Oxford University Press, 2015.

Lawless, Jennifer L., and Sean M. Theriault. "Sex, Bipartisanship, and Collaboration in the US Congress." Political Parity. Retrieved October 2016. https://www.politicalparity.

org/wp-content/uploads/2016/03/Sex_ Bipartisanship_Collaboration.pdf.

Left Foot Forward. "Why Rwanda Has the Most Female Politicians in the World." Retrieved October 2016. https://leftfootforward. org/2013/09/rwanda-has-the-most-female-politicians.

Madsen, Susan, ed. *Women and Leadership Around the World*. Charlotte, NC: Information Age Publishing, 2015.

Malcolm, Ellen R. *When Women Win: Emily's List and the Rise of Women in American Politics*. Boston, MA: Houghton Mifflin Harcourt, 2016.

Mount Holyoke College. "Readings in Proportional Representation." PR Library. Retrieved October 2016. https://www.mtholyoke.edu/acad/polit/damy/prlib.htm.

Mullainathan, Sendhil. "Racial Bias, Even When We Have Good Intentions." *New York Times*, January 3, 2015. http://www.nytimes.com/2015/01/04/upshot/the-measuring-sticks-of-racial-bias-.html?_r=0.

Name It, Change It. "An Examination of the Impact of Media Coverage of Women Candidates' Appearance." Retrieved October 2016. http://www.nameitchangeit.org/page/-/Name-It-Change-It-Appearance-Research.pdf.

BIBLIOGRAPHY

Nelson, Alyse. *Vital Voices: The Power of Women Leading Change Around the World.* New York, NY: Jossey-Bass, 2012.

Newton-Small, Jay. *Broad Influence: How Women Are Changing the Way America Works.* New York, NY: Time Books, 2016.

Newton-Small, Jay. "Women Are the Only Adults Left in Washington." *Time*, October 16, 2013. http://swampland.time.com/2013/10/16/women-are-the-only-adults-left-in-washington.

Packer, George. "The Quiet German: The Astonishing Rise of Angela Merkel, the Most Powerful Woman in the World." *New Yorker*, December 1, 2014. http://www.newyorker.com/magazine/2014/12/01/quiet-german.

Pew Research Center. "Raising Kids and Running a Household: How Working Parents Share the Load." November 4, 2015. http://www.pewsocialtrends.org/2015/11/04/raising-kids-and-running-a-household-how-working-parents-share-the-load.

UN Women. "Facts and Figures, Leadership and Political Participation." Retrieved September 2016. http://www.unwomen.org/en/what-we-do/leadership-and-political-participation/facts-and-figures.

Walkman, Michael. *The Fight to Vote.* New York, NY: Simon & Schuster, 2016.

Women's Media Center. "The Status of Women in the Media 2015." Retrieved October 2016. http://wmc.3cdn.net/83bf6082a319460eb1_hsrm680x2.pdf.

INDEX

A
Adams, Abigail, 10,11
Anthony, Susan B., 15

B
Bachelet, Michelle, 91
Baldwin, Tammy, 84
Biden, Joe, 27

C
Campbell, Kim, 20
Canada
 suffrage movement in, 17–18
 women politicians in, 8, 20, 22, 48, 77, 79
Caraway, Hattie Wyatt, 84
Center for American Women in Politics (CAWP), 87, 88
Chisholm, Shirley, 82
Clinton, Hillary, 4, 6, 25, 30, 49, 54, 55, 56, 58, 59, 60, 61, 79, 88, 90, 91, 92, 94
compromise, US Congress and, 63, 65–66, 69
consensus building, 66–68
critical mass, explanation of, 63, 65

D
Declaration of Sentiments, 4

E
economy, women leaders effect on, 72–73, 75–76
Emily's List, 40, 87

F
family, as hindrance to women governing, 26, 32–34, 58
Felton, Rebecca, 82
Fiorina, Carly, 59
France
 women oliticians in, 48
 women's suffrage in, 18

G
Gillibrand, Kirsten, 33
glass ceiling, 6, 8, 9, 24, 44, 61, 82, 91, 96
Germany
 political structure of government, 38
 women politicians in, 36, 48, 54
government shutdown of

109

2013, 63, 65–66
Green Party (Germany), 38
gross domestic product (GDP), women leaders and, 73, 75

I

implicit bias, 59–61
Italy, women's suffrage in, 18

K

Kelly, Megyn, 59

M

May, Theresa, 54
media jobs, women's representation in, 51–52
Merkel, Angela, 36, 54
Moseley Braun, Carol, 84
Mott, Lucretia, 12
multi-seat districts, 35, 40

N

National Organization of Black Elected Legislative Women, 88
New Zealand, women's suffrage in, 18
Nineteenth Amendment, 14, 17, 48

O

Obama, Barack, 6, 25, 36, 45

P

Palin, Sarah, 56, 58
pantsuits, 54–55
parliamentary system, 38, 40, 42, 46, 78
Pelosi, Nancy, 54, 56
Pierce, Charlotte Wood, 17
political consciousness, generational differences in, 91–92, 94, 96
political office, women in
 common traits of female leaders, 89, 91
 encouraging women to run by example, 42, 44
 firsts for women, 82, 84
 history of women running for, 18, 20, 22
 overcoming stereotypes, 46, 48–49, 51, 53
 reasons women don't seek office, 27–28, 30, 32–34
 scrutiny of physical

INDEX

appearance, 53, 56, 58
political system, structure of, 34–35, 38, 40, 42
proportional representation, 35, 38, 78
PTA method of legislation, 69

Q

quotas, for number of women in office, 79, 81, 84–85

R

Rankin, Jeanette, 48–49, 82
Rwanda, 70, 72

S

Sanders, Bernie, 53, 59
Seneca Falls Convention, 12, 14, 17
Shaheen, Jeanne, 65
She Should Run, 87
single-member districts, 35, 40
Stabenow, Debbie, 68–69
Stanton, Elizabeth Cady, 12, 18, 82
Switzerland, women's suffrage in, 18

T

training programs, 85, 87–88
Trudeau, Justin, 79
Trump, Donald, 53, 59

U

United Arab Emirates, women politicians in, 22, 89
United Kingdom, women politicians in, 48, 54
United Nations, 85
United States, percentage of women holding political office, 20, 22, 62

V

Vote Run Lead, 87
voting rates, women's, 23

W

Warren, Elizabeth, 44
Whitton, Charlotte, 49
Women's Campaign Fund, 40
women's suffrage, history of, 12, 14, 15, 17–18
Woodhull, Victoria, 18

111

ABOUT THE AUTHOR

When she was a senior in high school, Avery Elizabeth Hurt was president of her school's student government. She also spent many afternoons and weekends stuffing envelopes and licking stamps as a volunteer working for passage of the Equal Rights Amendment. She is the author of many books for children and young adults.

PHOTO CREDITS

Cover Kotin/Shutterstock.com; cover background STILLFX/Shutterstock.com; pp. 6-7, 52-53, 60 Bloomberg/Getty Images; pp. 11, 13, 16, 18-19 Everett Historical/Shutterstock.com; p. 21 PonoPresse/Gamma-Rapho/Getty Images; p. 23 Gabriel Olsen/Getty Images; pp. 28-29 Genaro Molina/Los Angeles Times/Getty Images; pp. 30-31 NurPhoto/Getty Images; p. 34 Jonathan Ernst/Getty Images; pp. 36-37 360b/Shutterstock.com; pp. 38-39 © AP Images; pp. 41, 67 Bill Clark/CQ-Roll Call Group/Getty Images; pp. 42-43 Chip Somodevilla/Getty Images; pp. 46-47 Asif Hassan/AFP/Getty Images; p. 50 Frank Lennon/Toronto Star/Getty Images; p. 55 Pool/Getty Images; p. 57 Marc Piscotty/Getty Images; pp. 64-65 Mandel Ngan/AFP/Getty Images; pp. 70-71 Amy Sussman/Getty Images; p. 73 Win McNamee/Getty Images; pp. 74-75 Pacific Press/LightRocket/Getty Images; pp. 80-81 arindambanerjee/Shutterstock.com; pp. 82-83 Owen Franken/Corbis Historical/Getty Images; pp. 86-87 Nation Media/Gallo Images/Getty Images; p. 90 Sean Gallup/Getty Images; p. 93 Boston Globe/Getty Images; pp. 94-95 Lintao Zhang/Getty Images; cover and interior pages (globe) LuckyDesigner/Shutterstock.com; cover and interior pages background designs lulias/Shutterstock.com, Dawid Lech/Shutterstock.com, Transia Design/Shutterstock.com.

Designer: Nicole Russo-Duca; Photo Researcher: Heather Moore Niver

3/18

SHIAWASSEE DISTRICT LIBRARY
32259007437688

324.082 HURT, AVERY
HUR WOMEN IN POLITICS

DISCARD

DATE DUE

NOV 8 2018

PRINTED IN U.S.A.